SHORTY

Blue

SHORTY

Blue

A NOVEL

R. Lee Walker

iUniverse®

SHORTY BLUE
A NOVEL

iUniverse books may be ordered through booksellers or by contacting:

iUniverse
1663 Liberty Drive
Bloomington, IN 47403
www.iuniverse.com
844-349-9409

Because of the dynamic nature of the Internet, any web addresses or links contained in this book may have changed since publication and may no longer be valid. The views expressed in this work are solely those of the author and do not necessarily reflect the views of the publisher, and the publisher hereby disclaims any responsibility for them.

Any people depicted in stock imagery provided by Getty Images are models, and such images are being used for illustrative purposes only. Certain stock imagery © Getty Images.

ISBN: 978-1-6632-3803-0 (sc)
ISBN: 978-1-6632-4571-7 (hc)
ISBN: 978-1-6632-3804-7 (e)

Print information available on the last page.

iUniverse rev. date: 09/29/2022

Contents

Preface vii

Prelude xi

Chapter 1 1

Chapter 2 5

Chapter 3 11

Chapter 4 17

Chapter 5 21

Chapter 6 25

Chapter 7 29

Chapter 8 35

Chapter 9 39

Chapter 10 45

Chapter 11 51

Chapter 12 55

Chapter 13 59

Chapter 14...63

Chapter 15...67

Chapter 16...71

Chapter 17...75

Chapter 18...79

Chapter 19...83

Chapter 20 87

Chapter 21...91

Chapter 22 95

Chapter 23 99

Chapter 24 103

Chapter 25 107

Chapter 26 111

Chapter 27 115

Chapter 28 119

Chapter 29 127

Epilogue..135

About The Author 139

Preface

R. Lee Walker

Shorty Blue is a fictitious story and any personality similarities are coincidental. In my opinion, everyone should have a legal will and a living trust. When property goes to probate it can cause ill feelings and family discord. This is why I wrote Shorty Blue.

As a child Shorty Blue overheard his mother say, "Doctor Rickett, Shorty is now thirteen years old and he looks like a midget. We feed him right, and I give him vitamins and he still won't grow. Ain't nobody short in this family." The doctor said, "Mrs. Blue all I can say is, when the time is right Shorty is going to shoot up over-night."

At fifteen-and-a-half, Shorty Blue started to grow, and he got so tall until nobody recognized him.

R. Lee Walker

Prelude

R. Lee Walker

The green rolling hills of Mississippi contrast against the yellow sky where the pine trees eclipse and cast a shadow on Shorty Blue's pensive and feverish mood. The old house that Shorty stayed in as a child was set back off the road about 300 feet on a slope; it was built during slavery and over 200 years old. So many memories are in that house that it's hard to know where to properly begin. Let's begin when Shorty's daddy died in 1954.

R. Lee Walker

Chapter

1

R. Lee Walker

Daddy was a medium, light brown-skin man with a short haircut and medium build. He loved to wear khaki shirts and pants, which were always clean because he wore an apron when he worked. Daddy looked mild and meek, but he was a fireball in church. He could pray and turn out the house. When it came time for Deacon Leroy to pray, he would put his right knee down and kneel, then bow his face to the ground and cut loose. "Oh God, help them," he would say.

Daddy was such a heavy prayer that we knew he would live forever. We figured that in order to pray like Daddy did, you had to be close to the Lord, and as a reward, would live long. When daddy died, Shorty's life was rocked. Daddy was a good man and to be honest, I don't think he was fully appreciated in our family and community as the force of nature that he was. He loved his family and worked very hard to support those he loved. Sadly, he never saw any of his kids accomplish anything on their own.

On the other hand, Mama was the opposite of Daddy. To the point that I sometimes wondered why they got married in the first place. It's not that they argued or anything; they just had starkly different interests. Mama took care of the home, while Daddy was out making the money that would pay the bills and put food on the table. They both worked hard in their respective ways. When it came time for Daddy and Mama to spend quality time, they went in different directions it seems they were better at being business partners than lovers.

When Daddy died, he left mom with all the property and deeds to the land. The family had over 300 acres of woods and grazing land. The landscape was beautiful, especially in the fall. It is this land that would be the bane and blessing of Shorty's existence.

Chapter

2

R. Lee Walker

Shorty Blue, whose real name was Kervin Lockhart, had three sisters and no brothers. Everybody always said that daddy and Shorty were just alike; according to family members, they were dead ringers. Like Daddy, Shorty had a medium-build, light brown-skin and he wore a short haircut. He also looked mild and meek, but if you crossed him, he was a fireball.

Shorty was the next to the oldest in the family. When his mother died, Shorty remembered leaving from his job on the railroad and going home. He looked forward to seeing his three sisters. Desiree was the oldest, Sherisse was next, then Phoebe. All his sisters were smart in school, but poor in choosing mates in a personal relationship. Not one of them was able to keep a man for long. They were all blessed with beauty; yet they had poor attitudes. Each had the same personality traits when they got angry.

No man would put up with that type of insult or behavior for long. Not only would they insult you, they would shade on the argument to disgrace your family roots, as if their family was superior. When Shorty's sisters attempted to attack him similarly, he found it best to just leave. But, sometimes, leaving was not the answer. Shorty learned soon enough that sometimes he had to stand up to his sisters and defend himself. *Otherwise, who would?* During Shorty's shift his supervisor told him to go back home. This not be a normal day.

The day Shorty went back home was not a normal day. The atmosphere of love was gone and there seemed to be division in the house. Mama had just passed away and the spirit of what he knew as home was empty. Her spirit was missing. The glue that held everything together was gone. The house was now just a shell with no substance. The core of essence was gone, never to return. A part of Shorty was gone and he didn't know how to find it. He would never again hear the sound of his mother's voice asking him, "Shorty, where are you?" Shorty knew that nobody – outside of his mother – cared for him, or at least, that is how he felt.

Shorty's mama was not even in the ground before his sisters started to fight over who gets what. Battle lines were drawn. The scene was unfortunate, seeing that all the sisters got along up until now. Who would have guessed that the Lockhart sisters, who once loved and cared for each other, would now become enemies? Shorty never thought he would hear Desiree say, "What about my future? What's mine is going to be mine. Momma knew what she wanted me to have." Desiree, was like a beauty queen with her light skin, long red hair, keen nose and long shapely legs. But, Desiree had a cunning, slick female voice, like a well-educated female attorney. "I'm a high-end person with a beer pocket book and I know it," she said.

Shorty's other sisters, Sherisse and Phoebe, had just as much interest as Desiree; they were upset, but at least, cordial.

Nothing was the same. The air was frigid, and a thick type of wind blew in one direction. The house on the hill seemed like nothing more than a backdrop of a distant cabin over the horizon. The idea that Mama had died was too much for Shorty.

Chapter

3

Before the burial of Shorty Blue's mother, there were issues to settle and the will had to be read. At the time of the reading of the will, Shorty was called out of town on a business trip because a train had derailed a few miles out of town. The railroad needed him to go and help prepare the rail lines. He stayed gone from home for about three weeks before returning. When Shorty returned, the will had already been read, and the parcels of land had been distributed.

Shorty asked Sherisse, "What did you do?"

Sherisse told Shorty that everything was taken care of.

"What does that mean?" Shorty asked.

She said everything was fine.

"It's not fine for me because I don't know what happened to mama's will," he said.

"Well everybody got what was coming to them," Sherisse said.

"Like what?" Shorty asked.

"I'm not telling. I don't want to talk about it; Mama is dead," she replied.

"Fine Sherisse, I'll find out."

Shorty awakened bright and early the next day, got in his truck, and made his way to the county hall of records to look up his mother's will. While at the office, he was able to look up his mother's will and saw all the provisions. He also noticed that his mother had willed him 100 acres of land. *So what happened to my land*, he thought. Shorty looked up the title deeds to the land maps and saw the latest transactions. He saw the transaction where he transferred rights from himself to sister Sherisse with his signature, which he never did. He could not believe what he saw. His signature was forged on the transfer document and deed. Shorty was hurt. His eyes became heavy and a cloud of depression covered his body. He felt cold, abandoned, and lonely. A world of darkness had engulfed him.

Shorty went to his truck and started the engine. He asked himself why someone would want to lie. He already knew that "money was the root of all evil." Someone felt that he didn't need the money. *But who forged his signature?* No one had his permission. He knew he would have to see an attorney and get legal advice on how to recover this situation. The problem was how much would it cost him.

He then asked himself, "Is it worth it?"

Why fight over a little patch of land? Why deal with all the confusion? Why have everybody in the family mad at me? How much is that patch of grass worth to you anyway? he thought.

So, Shorty went home to rest his mind and get some sleep. He was tired and frustrated. He realized that this was going to be a challenge, and no one would know just how much. Shorty knew it wouldn't be long before he found out. He needed a good night's rest.

R. Lee Walker

Chapter

4

The next morning, Shorty sat at the table expecting to see his sisters there. He wondered, *Which one of them sold me out? Which one of them didn't want me to have my share of the land?* He jokingly asked himself, *Who excluded the master?* It's the principal of the thing. Shorty knew he wouldn't steal from anyone, because his conscience just wouldn't allow it. He knew that all money wasn't good money. Blood money is dirty money. He wanted to enjoy spending his money. Stealing it in any form was not the way. When he looked at Phoebe, Desiree, and Sherisse, they seemed different to him and he wondered what gene pool they had come out of because none of them were like him.

Phoebe seemed to be the greediest sister of the Lockhart clan. Shorty had never known her to give anything away, as she wanted everything for herself. He figured it was Phoebe who forged his signature. He wanted to know outright but decided to wait. He remembered Phoebe saying, "Shorty, you are doing so well on the railroad that you don't need any money."

"Just because my job is good, I've got to watch my budget," he said in response.

Shorty spent so much on the road because he had to pay for his own meals and hotel stays, things his sisters didn't consider. There was nobody to help him. Shorty thought that maybe it is better to just find an attorney to help him and not say anything to his sisters. He knew that the more he said, the worse it would get.

R. Lee Walker

Chapter

5

R. Lee Walker

Shorty did not know what attorney to use. There were only three attorneys in town. He knew the news would get out all over town and it would be a big mess. There was no other way. Not only did he need an attorney, he needed a counselor as well, a person who could advise him on what to do. He was dealing with a family mess. He knew the church would run with the football. They would say it is a sin to sue his mother's will or estate, and others would say to let the matter alone. In Shorty's mind, it was the principle of the thing. All the land was full of woods and near a storage clearing. Deep in the back, late at night, companies were dumping their toxic waste. The land could be considered worthless. *So why fight over it*, Shorty thought? Again, it was the principle of the thing. This scenario ran through his mind over and over again.

Shorty felt that nothing should be taken away from him. This was his right. His mother loved him, too. He knew that if he let his sisters get away with this scam, he would not be able to undo it. He was determined to find the right lawyer to help him. The problem was where to find a good real estate attorney. He wanted someone who would not sell him out. Lawyers were so crooked. They would sometimes conspire among themselves to raise the fees so high that the plaintiff loses and nobody wins. Just like divorce lawyers. He would have to take that chance because he wanted what was his.

Shorty needed an attorney. His mother had passed away and left him what she wanted him to have. It was only fair that he got what was left for him.

Chapter

6

The family was preparing to go to the mortuary. Everybody was sad and tried to hide it. No one wanted to see this day. This is something everyone pushed out of their minds; but Mama died, and they all had to deal with it. The limousines came rolling up to the front of the house. It was mid-afternoon and everyone was ready to go to the wake. Phoebe had on her white embroidered dress with black shoes. Everybody was dressed really nice. Shorty had on black slacks and a pull-over sweater. He thought that was enough preparation for an event that was private. Nobody was going to be there but the family. It still was no excuse not to be dressed nicely.

Everybody loaded up into the limousine to head to the mortuary. The long black limousine was filled with all of the Lockhart children. The ride did not take long, and they arrived in less than 20 minutes. They were the only ones there. No other family members or friends arrived. Walking in was too much for everybody to handle. The thoughts that ran through everybody's head and the stress of the moment were too much for them to endure. Their emotions were exposed, and nobody could hold back their feelings. They could not recreate those feel-good family moments. They had to face reality. This was it.

The mortuary was a clean and cold place. A gentleman sat at a white desk situated near the far rear of the room. He stood up and escorted everyone to where Mama was lying-in-state. They walked into the room and gracefully saw the remains of their mother. Their hearts plummeted and tears began to flow. Now was the time to let them out and they did. Shorty knew his tears were not going to stop there. He knew, for months and Sundays, that he would cry in his sleep over the loss of his mother. Everybody was sober and sad. They stayed at the mortuary for two hours and talked to cover up their pain.

The next day was the funeral and about 200 people attended. The family did not want the service to be long, so every aspect was short and to the point. The speakers had to limit their comments to two minutes and nobody did, of course. The ride to the cemetery was the most grueling, but at least it was on site. When everyone departed, the reality of not having mama set in. The real adjustment period was about to begin.

Chapter

7

After the funeral Shorty demanded that the will be pulled and re-read with everybody there. The second reading of the will would take place on the next Saturday morning at Attorney Johnson's office. It was important that all the family would be there. Shorty knew this would be a critical moment. Everyone was ready. Attorney Johnson's office was a typical attorney's office, full of basic law journals of the state, federal, and tax codes. All attorneys have their degrees posted on their walls and special awards from the communities that they've served. Many of them have their family graduation pictures, in order to connect with their clients better. Attorney Johnson was a fat man with a deep voice. To Shorty, he was more a country preacher: a Pentecostal preacher with a humming voice.

Everyone sat around the office in hardwood chairs. Shorty's sisters were dressed in dark blue business attire. Attorney Johnson took the will out of his safe and began to read:

I blessed all my property to my children. One fifth of my property goes to all my children. There is an addendum ... Shorty, your fifth has been quitclaimed by you to your sister, Phoebe.

Shorty said, "What?" I did not quitclaim anything! Who told you that?"

"Here it is right here," Johnson said.

"No, there must be a mistake."

"Here is your signature... right here."

"This is not my signature," Shorty said. "Someone forged my signature. I'm going to have to file a lawsuit to correct the problem. Will you help me?"

"I can't Shorty! I have a conflict of interest; you must find an outside attorney."

"I will find an attorney. I can't let this stand," he said. Minutes later, the meeting with Attorney Johnson came to an end.

Later, Shorty confronted Phoebe about his forged signature.

"Shorty, you shouldn't be so upset," Phoebe said. "You got a job. You work for the railroad. You get benefits. We have nothing in this small town. Let the property go."

"Hell no! Did you forge my signature?" he asked heatedly.

"No," Phoebe replied.

"Then who did?" he asked.

"I don't know," Phoebe replied.

Shorty was stressed behind Phoebe's attitude. He knew Phoebe was not the only one to think like that, and it was time he found an outside lawyer and had his property cleared up and his title returned.

Shorty went to the next nearby town to find an attorney, and he did. He found an attorney and explained the situation and went to court to have that fraudulent deed reversed. However, in order to do that, he had to sue everyone in his family to have all the deeds reissued. He knew the family would be angry, and his name would be dragged through the mud. Just the idea of everybody going to court was enough to cause resentment and animosity; but the longer Shorty waited, the worse it would be for him. So he had to move fast. Shorty was vigilant in his efforts. The lawsuit was filed.

Just as Shorty thought, the family was angry with him. They said, "Shorty, you are greedy. You don't need any money ... Just let things alone. Don't take us through this ... So what, someone forged your name, you still can make it... You got a job and we don't. The property is not worth anything, anyway." He thought about how, when and why anyone would want to lie and steal what his mother wanted him to have. Shorty really thought Desiree was the main one who would give him some kind of problem with his mother's will, based on her ways, but when he went to examine the will at the Hall of Records, it was Sherisse who had Shorty's rights.

Phoebe had a quitclaim for Shorty's land specifically. This is why Sherisse didn't want to talk about the will and Phoebe tried to convince Shorty why he should just leave it alone, and let the land go. They knew they were wrong by forging Shorty's name and presuming that he wouldn't say anything about it. Shorty felt what was his, was his, and he wanted his day in court.

Chapter

8

The hearing was set for a Wednesday afternoon at 1:30 p.m. in the downtown municipal court building, room 300. The court was going to rule on the documents and reissue the deeds and verify Shorty's signature. He had no motive to take any of the property that was not his. The judge was an older Black female and she seemed to be a passive-type person. She had a straight face and strained, perceiving eyes. Her courtroom was one of discipline and order. It was as if the court was trained to run by itself.

"All rise," said the bailiff. "The honorable Judge Johanson has entered the court, please rise."

"My first case is Shorty Blue. Please come, approach the bench."

"All persons raise your right hand and repeat after me, 'I solemnly swear to tell the truth, the whole truth and nothing but the truth so help you God.'"

"I do."

"Please be seated."

"State your name for the court."

"My name is Shorty Blue."

"State your case."

"Somebody forged my name on a quitclaim deed. I don't know whose signature that is, and I did not give anybody my permission to use my signature or take my property."

"Fine, Mr. Blue. Does anybody object to canceling this fraudulent deed? If there are no objections, this deed is canceled, and reissued to the said Shorty Blue. This hearing is dismissed."

"I knew the judge was going to rule in your favor, Shorty," Phoebe said. "Shorty, you can't be mad at anyone because you got a job, we are all poor down here. We don't have anything and you've got your railroad job. That little piece of property in the scheme of things isn't that important, Shorty. I would have just let things alone."

"I know you would say something like that because it is not your property being taken," Shorty said. "It's mine. I want what Mama gave me. I have a right to it, just like you have a right to your portion. So, I am not going to feel bad about what is right. I've got to fight for what is mine. Mama told me if you don't fight to keep what is yours, you don't deserve to have it. So, I'm going all the way."

Phoebe dropped her head, then said, "Some things are better left alone. I know you wanted your share; even if you didn't know you had property coming, your life would remain the same."

"I know, but I got my portion of the property back, just like I was supposed to."

Chapter

9

R . Lee Walker

After a good night's sleep, the new day was overcast and misty. It was a nice autumn day. It was also a rite of passage, in the mind of Shorty Blue. Summer was nowhere in sight. He did what he had to do. His sisters had an attitude about his going to court to get his deed. None of them wanted to complain, but they wished he had left things alone.

Shorty always remembered his mom saying, "Women are money-hungry.

You can't trust them, Shorty," his mom once said. "They will set you up to get your money and literally will hang you out to dry. You've got to hide your money. People don't love any more. Life is about what you've got to offer."

Those words resonated in Shorty's mind. He knew it's hard being married these days. Seemed married couples wanted to get out and get a divorce. Single people marry to get married. The world is completely topsy-turvy or upside down. It made him wonder if there were any happy, married couples. Shorty felt it was alright to be single. It was best that a person hide their money than to expose it to the gold digger who would play him by pretending to love him and take his fortune. Shorty realized that people change and grow apart over the years. He knew that money had to be accounted for, but at what cost? Even with this in mind, Shorty was glad that he won his case.

Shorty was in the kitchen when the doorbell rang. Phoebe went to answer it. It was her boyfriend, Booker. Booker was a tall, light-skinned Black man with a pointed nose and green eyes. He wore a black tee shirt with jeans and a gold watch. He had a silver chain in his right belt loop with a rabbit's foot. He came into the house and went straight into the kitchen.

"Well Shorty, you won your case. Are you happy now?"

"Why did you ask me that? What business is it of yours?" Shorty asked.

"It's everybody's business," Booker said. "Look at the inconvenience you caused for your family. You should have left things alone."

"You mean, just let my portion be lost. Just let that fraudulent signature stand?"

"Yea mother fucker! Me and Phoebe could have leased out your parcel," Booker said.

"Are you sick, Booker? That parcel is not yours, it's mine!"

"Fuck you, Shorty. You need your ass beat!" Booker reached over and struck Shorty on the jaw, then yanked his right arm. They were fighting in the kitchen. They were choking each other. They were wrestling on the floor and no one stopped them. While all this was going on, the mailman called the police to come out and stop the altercation. The police came and stopped the fight and both of them went to jail to sort out the problem. Shorty knew it was time for him to go.

R. Lee Walker

Chapter

R. Lee Walker

Shorty was injured by the violent encounter. His right leg muscle was strained and his back felt dislocated. He walked with a limp. That fight left a bitter taste in his mouth about everything. The town, his mother's house, and his sisters no longer had anything to offer him. He wanted out. He wanted to leave. He wanted to go as far as he could to get away from Mississippi.

To Shorty, it did not make sense for Booker and his family to be angry at him for asking for his share of the property. He knew that the parcels could be leased out or rented to the government for land enrichment programs. Just the thought that someone wanted to fight him about his own property did not make any sense.

Shorty knew his greedy sister, Phoebe, and her boyfriend, Booker, wanted him out of the way. Shorty felt times were hard everywhere. He wanted more adventure, and all his other relatives were in Chicago, but he didn't want to go there. He thought about moving west. California would be new territory. California would be far enough where his family roots could not follow. He could work for Southern Railroad in Los Angeles as a porter. Now was the time to move out west. After the big fight, he started to prepare himself for the transition. There was nothing to hold him back. He did not have a girlfriend or anyone he was interested in, or who was interested in him. So why not move?

The train ride to Los Angeles took two days. Shorty looked forward to the journey. He knew that working the Star Line from Los Angeles to Oregon would be fun and different. But first, he had to get to Los Angeles to get situated. That town was all spread out into regions. Los Angeles had a very poor transportation system. At that time, they had a few rail lines and streetcars. Buses were very slow. This city was really a cow town compared to New York and other eastern cities. Shorty knew there were a lot of Baptist churches and Pentecostal preachers waiting to take his money, which was fine. He felt society needed religion to keep the family unit together. But he knew it would be some time before he would find a church home. All these premonitions were in Shorty's mind before he arrived in Los Angeles. In just a few hours, he would actually be there.

The train arrived at Union Station. No one was there to meet him and he didn't have anywhere to go. That was the hard part. Everyone needed family and friends. It was a beautiful, sunny day. The train station was busy with a lot of people rushing to their destinations. Shorty did not know the town or where to find a hotel. So naturally, the thing to do was take a taxi to the Black side of town and find a motel. The taxis were located outside Union Station and the one he found took him to 23rd and Central Avenue in the center of Los Angeles, not far from downtown.

It was a simple motel and very clean. Shorty did not have much in terms of luggage, just two suitcases and one tote bag. He knew material things would come, causing his space to become cluttered. In order to get a room, he stood outside the window and completed the application. He told the attendant he would like to stay for a while, at least a month in order to get himself situated. The attendant told him that the rooms were nice and clean and they all had telephones. This is just what Shorty needed in order to contact Phoebe back in Mississippi to find out how everything was going. Shorty's new life was beginning.

Chapter

11

R . Lee Walker

The next day, Los Angeles was hot, dry and smoggy. The gray sky and dirty air quality was too much, but Shorty had never experienced a city's climate like that before. He had heard about California being humid but being in an environment where you could not breathe and being expected to work was unreal. Shorty wanted to call back home to tell Phoebe and the others that he was alright and made it to Los Angeles safely. The thoughts of the fight with Booker and his family still ran in his mind. Just the idea that anyone would be mad at him for trying to protect what was legally his, did not make any sense.

He loved the land in Mississippi. He loved the winding country roads and the open green pastures. He loved looking over the lakes and watching the moon shining and so many stars in the sky in the evening; and for him to be alive in this universe was a thrill in itself. He thought about how people get so tied up in personal affairs that they forget what life is really all about. The old preacher from his hometown church used to say, "Life is about serving God and helping others." That was the problem. When it comes to helping others, who are the people that appreciate your help. He visualized his mother who always said, "When a person shows you who they really are, believe them." To him, that meant don't overlook the signals a person is giving you. If you do, problems begin.

Shorty called back home and no one was there. He left the motel to find a restaurant where he could have breakfast. He had a taste for waffles and eggs, and a good cup of coffee. When he returned from the restaurant, there was a message on his telephone. The telephone service told him to call home and that it was an emergency. He could only wonder, *what now? What could Phoebe want?* He called Phoebe late that night and found out the news.

"Shorty," Phoebe said. "Something is happening to your property that the court awarded you. It is your property, Shorty. Only on your property did they find oil. They say it's a lot of it. That means you're rich, Shorty and you can help all of us!"

"I don't know about all of that," Shorty said. "I have to find out about what is going on, regarding land rights and mineral rights under the ground. I've got to call the banker to establish lease rights and hire an attorney to protect my interest. Phoebe, there is a lot for me to do. I'm just getting started. Let me make some calls before I come back home to take care of my business.

Chapter

12

R . Lee Walker

The next morning, Shorty called the community banker. Ben Price was the bank president. As he spoke, Ben began to congratulate him on his success.

"Congratulations, Mr. Blue. You are now a rich man. It is no telling how much oil is on your land! Are you ready to sign a lease agreement for shipping, selling and what have you?"

"Sir, I don't know. I'm going to have to take the train back there to figure this out."

"No Shorty, no train. You can fly on us," Ben Price said. "You need to come immediately and stay at a nice hotel in town. I don't know about staying with your relatives, there might be too much pressure."

"I think you are right," Shorty said.

Shorty went to the manager of the hotel where he was staying and told him that he was checking out. The manager said, "You just got here."

"I know, but there is some pressing business that I must handle, and I must leave." Later that day, Shorty received his fare sent via special delivery through Western Union to return home to Mississippi.

He took a taxi to Los Angeles International Airport. He was flying Delta Airlines down south. This was the first time Shorty had ever been on an airplane, and he was scared. He did not want anybody to know that it was his first time flying. However, in his mind, he kept thinking: *What if this plane crashes? What am I going to do?* Then he rationalized with himself, "My life is not my own." He knew he'd be lying to God if he said he wasn't going to worry anymore.

His flight took about five hours. He changed planes in Dallas/ Fort Worth. He took a Continental flight to Jackson, Mississippi. When he arrived in Jackson, there was a private limousine waiting for him. The limousine took him straight to the hotel. Nobody but the manager of the bank knew he was in town.

R. Lee Walker

Chapter

13

R. Lee Walker

The sun was warm, but the air was cool on that warm autumn day in mid-October. Shorty went straight to the bank that afternoon to meet with Mr. Price. Ben Price was a heavy set, middle-aged white man with a pleasant smile. He welcomed Shorty into his office and began to explain what was happening on the property and the exploratory findings. Mr. Price had the legal description and a copy of the court rulings that gave sanction to Shorty's ownership in the property. Price told Shorty about the company that would extract the oil and the one that would refine it. Shorty asked if he could have his attorney review the documents, prior to signing the agreements. The bank told him to take his time.

Shorty took the documents and contacted his family lawyer for an appointment later that day. He used the same attorney that handled his mother's will. He felt confident that his interest would be protected. Later that evening, he went to the office of the attorney to discuss the mineral leases.

"So, Mr. Johnson, what does all this mean?" Shorty asked the family attorney.

"It means that you are very wealthy. There is nothing you can't have."

"I know that! Especially if you own your very own oil well," he said.

▲ ▼ ▲ ▼ ▲ ▼

Booker and Phoebe argued back at his mother's house. Booker was adamant that someone needed to bump off Shorty, so they would have his money.

"I told you that there was oil or something on that land somewhere, because the ground smelled so bad at night," Booker said. "Let's find out where he is and have someone kill him. We can pay somebody to do it."

"I don't want my brother killed," Phoebe said.

"Why not, God damn it? What has he done for you? Get rid of his ass. I should have accidentally killed his butt when we got in the fight before the funeral," Booker said. "Look Phoebe, I don't have a God damn thing in life. I don't have a pension from service; I don't have any property. But I can have something through you. You and I can pull together. We can have a grip in life and be somebody. All we have to do is knock off your brother by surprise and split his land as next of kin. It's simple. He doesn't have any children, wife, or a girlfriend. Let's just get rid of his ass. When it comes to money, I would get rid of my mama, daddy, and almost anyone except you Phoebe. You know I love you. We need to find out where Shorty is. He has to come back to town to handle his business. When we find him, we can set him up some kind of way, or pay someone to shoot him and knock him off."

Chapter

14

R. Lee Walker

S horty concluded the meeting with his attorney. The papers were in order. He was going to return them to the bank the next day. He was going to sign a 99-year lease with Standard Oil and have the checks sent to his local bank in Mississippi, then wired to the bank in Los Angeles. He needed a beneficiary, but he didn't know whom to name at the time. His health was good, but it could change without notice. He did not want his family members to know he was in town. After his business meeting, he flew back to Los Angeles and returned to the same motel. Even though his circumstances had changed, Shorty still wanted to play the role of being broke and barely making it to protect himself from gold diggers and con men.

Los Angeles was a different kind of place. Central Avenue was jumping just like New Orleans. There were blues clubs up and down the streets. The core of the city in Los Angeles was black. There were soul food restaurants everywhere. There were liquor stores and churches on every corner. When you left South Central Los Angeles, you could not find a liquor store for miles. There were street gangs because the unemployment was high. At night, the street came alive and all the people came out for a good time. What little money they had, they were willing to spend on fun. The Dunbar Hotel was the place for Jazz and Rhythm & Blues. Some famous musicians such as Diana Washington, Sara Vaughn, Billy Eckstein, and Ray Charles would come through. There was nothing of interest in the Hollywood area but tourists from out of town. The Melrose area had a lot of Jewish jewelry stores, antique stores, and delicatessens. The Westwood area was a college town because of the University of California, Los Angeles. There were a lot of movie houses and restaurants to enjoy.

Shorty learned later about Venice Beach. That area became his favorite hangout. People there were cool and intellectually, free thinkers. Nowhere in the South was there any place like Venice Beach.

Chapter

15

R. Lee Walker

Phoebe and Booker saw the oil wells on Shorty's property and could not stand the idea that he was rich. They wondered what he was doing with all that money. He is not married, he didn't have any kids, he was not gay, didn't gamble, so he must be saving the money for property or something. Booker had friends that were like him. They would rob and kill for a dollar if they could get away with it. He needed to know where Shorty lived in Los Angeles to set him up. That way, if they off Shorty, his property would fall to the next of kin.

Booker told Phoebe that he loved her and wanted the best for her. He said Shorty stood in the way of them living the good life. In Booker's mind, Shorty's land should belong to them. Shorty had no idea that his family was plotting to take his property. He had no idea that they were money hungry like that. He knew that certain people were jealous of him, but not to the point where they'd commit murder.

Meanwhile in Los Angeles, Shorty was continuing to check out the communities. Most Black people were hard working folks. They went to church on Sundays and had dinner afterwards. There were lots of board and care shelters for the homeless and elderly. Los

Angeles was not a perfect town because it was so spread out. Shorty also noticed that the police department was very prejudiced against Black men. Everywhere Shorty went, he noticed that only Black men were being arrested. In a big town like Los Angeles, why were black men the only men committing crimes? The police force appeared to be made of predominately white men. Shorty wanted no part of law enforcement or any social problems. Although he was concerned about civil rights, he felt that mandate wasn't everyone's passion. There could be no justice if there was no peace in the community.

Chapter

16

R . Lee Walker

After meditating, Shorty decided not to return to the railroad. There was too much going on. The confusion with the will, the sudden change in status, the attitudes in the family toward him, all of it was a little much to digest at one time. He did not know he was going to be wealthy overnight. He couldn't have imagined this in his wildest dreams. Just the idea of leaping into unknown boundaries and inheriting oil was too much to fathom.

He was aware of the gold diggers who would try to take his money and his life if he wasn't careful. He knew he could be flamboyant and decided to maintain a low profile. He felt that if he was going to spend some money, he needed to spend it abroad or at least out of state so he wouldn't be a target of suspicion. His mother told him that he should not trust people farther than he could see them. That paranoia was buried deep in his subconscious and in his heart. Maybe that's why he thought he could not maintain a serious relationship.

While working for the railroad, he saw families that appeared to be unified. There were mothers and fathers who spent quality time with their children. You could tell that there was love and respect in their homes. Often times these families were Christian-based. He often thought, *if only he could have a family like that*; his sisters especially. Phoebe was desperate for a man. She would sacrifice her love for her family just to keep a no-good man like Booker in her life. Sure, Shorty could afford to seek out love, but Shorty remembered hearing a rich man say on television, "Money does not buy happiness but it helps me pursue my goals."

Shorty thought he had many goals. *Now, all I need is ample time on this planet to do all the things I want to do. Some people want to be rich, but now I'm already rich, so now my dreams must be fulfilled. I still need to work. I will just move from this motel into a quiet place and become a commodity broker.* Shorty thought of collecting cans and bottles and having a truck to help him double his money. Shorty chose to move into an alley on Forty-Fifth Street and Avalon Boulevard in a back house. He would be safe from the general public.

Chapter

R. Lee Walker

While staying at the hotel, Shorty used to leave his room and walk around to survey the area. He noticed all the trash being thrown away: Big bags of cans, bottles, and scrap metal. To him, it did not make any sense. He took a bus and traveled the city on different trash days and saw the same old thing: People were throwing away valuables. He felt if folks would open their minds and stop being so wasteful, society and the environment would be much better off. While out one day, Shorty thought *what if I got a truck and an old shopping basket and wore some old clothes? I could salvage those valuable items. I could get me a dog to fight off the stray dogs and cats while I check the alleys.*

What Shorty did not know was society looked down upon people who appeared poor and down on their luck. He did not know that kids would throw rocks at him and call him out of his name. In Los Angeles, anyone who lived on the streets was ridiculed. Over time, Shorty would find this out.

Scrap iron and metal recycling would be a lucrative business. Now it was just finding a yard to get started. Shorty learned the recycling yards were on the East side of town, behind City Hall, near the railroad tracks. He needed to make contact with the businesses to establish his accounts. Shorty met with the business owners of the salvage yards and found out the exchange rates for the scrap metals and bottles. Most of the yards had a compressor for the metal and he knew that the salvage business would grow and become lucrative because of the high demand for the alloy.

Back in Mississippi, Phoebe and Booker could not locate Shorty. They wanted to find him to figure out what was going on in Shorty's life. They wanted to know where the money was going. How was he spending it? They visited the oil field and they saw the men working the pumps. They knew that Shorty was getting paid. Booker's conscience was bothering him. He wished he had killed Shorty when he had the fight. He could have kept that fraudulent deed and became rich, but that did not happen. However, in his mind, it still wasn't too late. He needed to find Shorty to arrange for something to happen and Phoebe could collect as next of kin. Phoebe and Booker were the only ones in the family who had that greedy and travois attitude. They wanted something for nothing.

Booker never wanted to work or hold a job. All he wanted to do was gamble and hustle. Phoebe was willing to work, but she had low self-esteem. She did not love herself, but she liked the attention Booker gave her. She thought Booker was exceptional with her. To her, Booker was a rebel without a cause. Booker was one to stand up to the system and say, "Hell no." Yes, Booker was her type of man. How far could she get with a man like Booker? Who knew? Whatever Booker wanted, Phoebe wanted too. Booker and Phoebe were a team. Their job was to find Shorty and get his money as quickly as possible.

Chapter

18

Shorty moved from the motel on Central Avenue to the back alley house. This was a good location because he could come and go from the alley without being noticed. People were too busy to care about commercial trucks and vagrants pushing shopping carts this way. No one would ever suspect that he was a wealthy man. He noticed that people in the city threw away valuable items that could be sold and recycled. It seemed like nobody cared. If only folks would open their minds and stop being so wasteful, they would have more money in their pockets. To Shorty, this city offered opportunity. People were too proud to think outside the box to make money and save money. He remembered one of his sisters would not be seen in a nickel-and-dime store. She would say people would think she was "down on her luck."

Shorty would say, "If you are not rich, you are down on your luck." The best way to help the poor is to not be one of them. The money from his estate was coming in. He had his checks coming to his new location. He immediately cashed them in and put the money into a money order because the checks were only good for so long. He saved enough money to buy himself an old truck to haul the rubbish. He went to the City Department of Sanitation to find out what days the city picked up trash. He would survey the area the night before and pluck out the valuables.

People would see him pushing his cart with a dog by his side and felt sorry for him. He always wore a blue shirt and dark blue pants so much so that the school children would yell out while seeing him pushing his cart, "Here comes Shorty Blue." People saw Shorty Blue all over the city, especially in the early morning collecting cans, bottles and other items. He would load all the items on his truck and cash them in.

The dichotomy was that Shorty was a wealthy man with an oil well in his backyard and money in the bank and yet, he still wanted to collect bottles. Was it for even more personal gain, wealth and value? What went on in Shorty's mind that possessed him to minister and connect with people that way? There were times when school kids would throw rocks at him and hit Shorty's dog. One time. Shorty threw a rock back and hit a kid in the head. The kid went to school and complained to his teacher and she called the police. The police later stopped Shorty for questioning, but the authorities could not prove it was him who threw the rock. After questioning, they released him. Shortly after, people in the community began to recognize him as a staple in the neighborhood.

"Here comes Shorty Blue," they'd say. "He does not mess with anybody, so let him alone."

Chapter

19

R. Lee Walker

As the days and months passed, Shorty became wealthier. He was not spending his money on anything. He still did not have a girlfriend or wife. He was living the simple life. On Sunday mornings, he would go to church. He visited a lot of churches. It depended on the mood he was in. He liked sanctified churches because they were alive. The people moved around singing and dancing in the Spirit. Then there were churches like the science of mind. The people were quiet. The leader would just talk to you about personal motivation.

Shorty wanted to find an organization that was about the people and serving God, not just about the money. He wanted to be part of a group that was contributing to the community. He wanted to help the elderly and the orphan children in half way houses around the city and the world. He believed God blessed him for a purpose and there was a reason for everything. He heard that to whom much is given, much is required. He knew that it was in the Bible, but he did not know where. He did not want to be wasteful with his gift God had given him. He did not want to be flamboyant or attract attention from the wrong kind of people. He wanted to maintain a low profile. He wanted people to want him for who he was, not what he could do for them.

He just did not need gold diggers in his life. He knew gold diggers were superficial. In relationships with gold diggers, there is no love, no purpose, and no help. Life was too short to live without purpose. Life is a matter of the heart and what kind of heart a person has. Now that he had money, his dream was to hold on to it. If his oil well was to go dry tomorrow, then what?

In the meantime, he could give some money away as a tax shelter. He needed to find a local attorney to set up a foundation to help others in need. Now Shorty's mind was becoming clear. He could maintain a low profile and find a church or an organization to support through his newly established foundation, and maybe even find a special woman to share his life, since he was in good health. The world was his to discover.

Chapter

20

R. Lee Walker

Shorty used to start out in the morning around 4:00 A.M. He used to park his truck on McKinley and Florence Avenues and walk with his shopping cart north on McKinley past 49th Street Elementary School. There were a lot of alleys and Monday was the trash pick-up day. Women used to slip outside in their gowns and slippers to dump the trash. To Shorty, there were pretty women all over the place. He wondered how many were married. He didn't know, but the desires of his heart kicked in. He thought to himself, *if I could be on this street at the same time, over time I would see this pretty woman again.*

There was a pretty lady with light complexion at Victory Baptist Church on 48th Street and McKinley. She lived in a green house near the corner. She was Shorty's fantasy. He saw her close up one time and her spirit made him melt. She looked Puerto Rican or Spanish. It did not matter. He wanted to know her, but he knew that while he was looking like a vagrant, he would not have much of a chance with her. He realized he needed to be two people. He could be the street man and the businessman. In his mind, he knew most people would not want to associate with a bum. They would just look and walk the other way. Shorty realized he needed a dual identity to be able to associate with those in the upper echelons of society.

Even though he wanted to hide his money from the gold diggers, what good was it if he could not enjoy it? He remembered his mother saying, "You came to this world with nothing and you will leave with nothing." Shorty made up his mind that he was going to treat himself. He decided to call a taxi and take a flight to Las Vegas and stay at the finest hotel and enjoy a whirlpool tub for two people. Life is too short and money is no good if you can't spend some of it. Why wait until others take it from you? He had the fantasy in his mind. If he could find a beautiful woman to soak with in a hot tub, and enjoy champagne on a quiet night in a beautiful room overlooking the city, that would be amazing. What a fantasy it would be: To get away knowing that the tantalizing arguments between lovers would be worth it. Just to get away, knowing all that he has been through would be a personal treat. As Shorty thought about it, he continued to convince himself that this was the right thing to do. Now, that is a payoff and something to look forward to.

Chapter

21

R. Lee Walker

Booker and Phoebe could not find Shorty. Booker had become obsessed with finding Shorty and in his mind, Shorty was public enemy No. 1. Booker wanted Shorty to turn over some of that land. In Booker's mind, he saw himself as an executive in New York City in a giant, high-rise office building. He felt that with Shorty's money, he could educate himself and hire lawyers to help achieve his goals. In his mind, money would make him somebody people would look up to. He wouldn't have to take a back seat if he had cash. *Money talks and bullshit walks.* He felt that he had to get to Shorty's money any way he could. His family always missed the boat. They never had the opportunity to succeed. The time was never right. Millions of dollars were close to slipping away. Phoebe had the land first and the court took her fortune randomly and awarded the title to Shorty.

Booker could not wait for the opportunity to undermine Shorty in some way. He knew Shorty would call home again and tell them where he was. Booker had the plan already in his mind. It was already worked out. Booker knew Phoebe. He knew she would do whatever he said because she was in love with him. When someone loves you, your faults are overlooked and the person is blinded and can do no wrong. Phoebe identified with Booker and she wanted Shorty's money, too. Booker was right in Phoebe's mind. Shorty did not need anything. He always had everything he wanted. The railroad job was a good job. It took him all over the country and paid him well. The Army took young men away and didn't pay them anything. And you may lose your life. The Army had some points. It allowed young men a chance to see how others lived and to mature. This was a good thing.

R. Lee Walker

Chapter

22

R. Lee Walker

Shorty had his days planned out. He knew what part of the city he was going to be traveling. He would always be there before trash pick up in wealthy, high-end areas that did not believe in going to the trash dump. They would leave valuables in the front of their houses for anyone who needed or wanted them. Shorty knew this and he had a field day. Some of the things people threw away were things people would kill for in other countries, like a stove or blanket to help make life easier.

Shorty was starting to make a good profit off of rubbish. Even though his bank account from the oil wells was increasing, he felt his disguise was best. It was interesting to watch how the city worked. He saw things most people didn't see. He would see a man leave for work in the morning then two hours later another man would show up at the same door. He saw the secret lovers that would show up: male and female. During the day, he even saw some cross-dressed men. Nothing bothered him because this was the excitement of the big city and in the big city you could find almost anything. There was so much deception in the city; even the way he was living was deceptive.

Shorty knew he wasn't poor, yet he was living as if he was. He was living a lie. What if he met someone he liked? She wouldn't know what to think. Shorty knew that a person must be able to reason or know the difference between the truth and a lie. This is what life is about: The balance between right and wrong. Once a person makes the distinction of what is right, he can make an agreement with himself. A person can determine the direction he or she wants his life to go. You never know a person by looking at the outside surface. Like with Shorty, you have to judge the mind.

Chapter

23

R. Lee Walker

Nobody in the city knew Shorty Blue. People would see him and simply look the other way. Once Shorty saw a father walking with his son, maybe talking with him about school, and the young boy said, "Look at that man, here he comes." The father replied, "Son, don't mess with people like that. There is something mentally wrong with him." When Shorty heard that, he immediately thought this was what most people probably thought when they saw him.

The main idea was to be low key in a big city. He was warned of the gold diggers. Just the idea of a woman with a lot of men who would lay a baby on him because she knew he had money and the others did not, kept Shorty on his toes. This was a class scenario. How could he prove that the child was his? Shorty knew he would be stuck for 20 years. He wanted to find a woman who had good work habits and a good attitude. With a good attitude comes values that are worthy of trust. There was only one woman in Mississippi who he knew like that. It was Lynda, his childhood sweetheart. She was pretty, intelligent and very smart. So what happened? Lynda went to college and Shorty went to work for the railroad. Somehow they didn't stay in touch. Somehow, once Lynda left his life, no other woman interested him.

Shorty felt it was hard sometimes, especially since he was a 42-year-old man, to control his urge to have sex. He wanted to find a good whore to take care of him. He knew he needed love, but sex would do. Is that always the case; where a man's physical desires for satisfaction comes first and the emotional desires come last? The idea of being alone in a huge city with nobody to call his, in a lonely room with no family on a rainy night, was too much. At least on the train tracks, he had the guys as family. Everybody played cards like Bid Wiz or Tonk, which were the games that were quick and fun. Everyone laughed and exchanged stories.

The porters on the train were well-educated. During that time, they would overhear business executives discuss business opportunities and prospective land deals. A lot of guys knew where to invest their money because of those conversations and sent their children to schools to get the best opportunities.

It is true that opportunities open doors to a better life? You have to be able to recognize an opportunity when it appears. You must believe in yourself and want the best for yourself. So you take advantage of the best opportunity. People will never be rich because they are too used to being poor. All of their friends are poor and they don't want to leave their friends. Shorty knew this philosophy did not apply only to material things but spiritually as well. Too much was happening in and around his life, and he wanted to take his time to figure things out.

Chapter

24

It was a cold, windy night in LA. Shorty was driving down Western Avenue near Manchester when his rear tire blew out. He pulled to the side of the road and saw a sign on a green building which read public shelter open. He decided to take a chance and walk over to see if they would harbor him for the night. It was starting to rain and he knew it would be difficult to find help. Before his tire blew out, Shorty was thinking how life was a chance and how relationships were a wide shot. You never know which relationship is going to work until you try it. He knew he wanted a person to want him for who he was and not for what he had to offer. Shorty was justified in maintaining a low profile. He walked over to the shelter and knocked on the door. A middle-aged Black man with white hair and a green shirt answered the door.

"Are you looking for a place to spend the night?" he asked.

"I am," Shorty replied.

"Well we have plenty of couches left," he said. "Come in."

There were small families inside. They were mostly homeless, but not prostitutes. The people were clean and not transients. Shorty went to the back of the facility and lied down on his couch. He was given a gray blanket to keep him warm. In the morning, the facility served a hot breakfast of grits, fresh eggs, ham and toast. While eating, Shorty saw a very appealing lady with brown hair sitting with two small children. He wondered how could a young woman so lovely be homeless. Could it be something was wrong with her?

"Hey miss, my name is Shorty; some people call me Shorty Blue," he said.

"Hi Shorty, I'm Janice and these are my kids, Robert and Joyce," she said. "I'm glad to meet you. We are waiting on our apartment to come through so we won't have to be in this shelter for too long. Where we stayed, the building was sold because it was in foreclosure and we had to leave."

"How long have you been a single mom?" Shorty asked.

"For about two years," Janice said. "My husband was in and out of jail on drug charges and we got divorced." Janice seemed to have the personality Shorty liked. Her kids seemed to be good kids and Janice was a devoted mom. She seemed to be a woman with Southern values. She seemed like a woman of her word. She looked you directly in the eyes when she spoke. Her tone of voice had sincerity and meaning like a determined gym coach directing her students. Shorty knew he would secretly help the woman and her children. The staff at the shelter was a nice group of people. Shorty also knew he would secretly support the shelter through his foundation. The next day, Shorty got help for his truck and departed for his apartment.

Chapter

25

R. Lee Walker

Nothing missed Shorty's sight. He saw drug deals and undercover police officers posed as drug buyers to set up local pushers. He saw how they met in the back alleys or blocks as a way to collect and plan their strategies. Of course, Shorty knew not to get involved or make friends with anyone doing a foul of the law. That is trouble that Shorty did not need. The criminal justice system for a black man is a disaster. You can't find decent representation and it is far too expensive and nobody is honest. The whole legal system is a racket.

Shorty consistently reminded himself that being in disguise would protect him from the sharks and gold diggers. This way, he could remain out of trouble and not be set up with another man's baby. Baby mama drama could happen to any man, anywhere. The cost of that stress could last for years, or almost a lifetime. When you have a good man in a court system that's designed to rule in the woman's favor, you have a problem that will drain you. Especially when they find out what you have.

With that in mind, he knew it was best to stay Shorty Blue. No one would know what assets he had. He could avoid being set up for money. By being low key, he could help people anonymously like the shelter he stayed in one night. He could send a check or money order in the mail for them. Shorty knew if the person was a Christian, they would say, "I got a check from God." By doing this, he would have control over money and not the opposite, and he could avoid a system that would make him pay for what he is not responsible for in life.

In a big city, you need a stream of income to survive, something that is dependable to pay the bills. Without that guaranteed income you are in a hit and miss situation; and without a partner or back up, you will suffer. He wanted to keep track of the people on the street who were nice to him so he could repay them for their kindness. Shorty was convinced a low profile was the best policy that would eliminate unwanted stress in his new life.

Chapter

26

R. Lee Walker

Phoebe had not heard from Shorty in weeks. Booker wanted to find Shorty because he was still obsessed with jealousy and envy. He just couldn't figure out where Shorty was living. He thought Shorty was living in a fine mansion and driving a Bentley or Rolls Royce. Booker imagined Shorty had rich white women, cooks, and maids around him. He imagined Shorty living the high life of the rich and famous. He knew owning an oil well could do this for him.

What Booker didn't know was that the opposite was true. Shorty was maintaining a low profile life. Shorty liked knowing the money was building up. He liked working the low end. He enjoyed the big city in the mornings before sunrise. It was cold in the winter but nice in the spring. The big city had so many opportunities. He passed all the restaurants and theaters. He observed the shops and churches where people gathered. He thought about the cities he visited while working for the railroad; each city had its own personality.

For Shorty, he liked cities where he could sit and look at the stars at night, gaze at the inclusiveness of the universe. Just to be alive in the majestic vastness of God was invigorating for him. His thoughts included urbanization as a good thing. The politics, transportation system, and schools were all examples of humanity at its best. He wanted to live clearly and not overspend. This was the way of God. People who flash their money would not have it long. Being discrete was the best policy.

That year, the Los Angeles Dodgers had signed Jackie Robinson to its team. Shorty wanted to see him play. He had never been to a baseball game before and decided he would go see the Dodgers. No matter what his family thought, Shorty was living a conservative life and did nothing outlandish.

R. Lee Walker

Chapter

27

R. Lee Walker

April was a good time of year. The flowers bloomed and the gardens were coming to life. Living poor but being rich gave Shorty a depth that most people didn't have. He knew that most people were emotional quicksand and that once he got involved with them, he'd be stuck. He did believe in sharing. He made a list of charitable organizations and people who he was going to help secretly. This way, he could benefit others and help himself. Shorty saw himself as an instrument of personal fulfillment of the person who had hope. He could now really help somebody.

Although he wanted to help others. Shorty had a hard time suppressing his own desires for physical affection. He craved companionship and the lust for love and sex occupied his heart and mind regularly. He knew he couldn't take money with him when he died, but love was an imprint that would last on his soul forever.

Most people, his family included, were clueless to how organized Shorty was. He wrote everything down and kept lists and journals. He would write down his priorities and remained committed to what he had written. With a mind and speech like his, he should have been working in a manufacturing plant somewhere.

Shorty became well-known in the neighborhood as more and more people would see him before trash day sifting through the garbage. Some people would get angry because they felt their trash was private. Others thought the items in their trash cans were worthless. Shorty learned much about the people in the various neighborhoods, based on the items they threw away. Too often, families would purchase products, such as wide-screen televisions and other luxury items that would display their value system and economic status. Some folks were very private and Shorty could tell because their trash didn't reveal too much about them. Shorty knew that, like dirty laundry, the trash would odor out and reveal the habits, interests and identities of these people, sooner or later.

Chapter

28

R. Lee Walker

While out on a gray Sunday morning on a well-manicured and lush street on the west side of Los Angeles, Shorty sorted through some of the trash cans lined neatly along the front curb. He wasn't new to the area and had canvassed the neighborhood several times before. As he sorted through the trash of one Spanish style house, he looked up to see police cars advancing toward him with officers pouring out of their vehicles with guns drawn. "Stop what you are doing!" one officer shouted through a megaphone. "You are under arrest."

"For what, officer?" Shorty asked.

"You have the right to remain silent. Anything you say can and will be held against you in the court of law. You have the right to an attorney and if you don't have one, an attorney will be provided for you."

"What have I done?" Shorty asked again.

"Burglary," the officer said.

"Who and where? Tell me what I burglarized?" Shorty questioned while the officers started to search his contraband.

"Let's take him downtown for booking," the officer said ignoring Shorty's questions. "Let's secure his dog and belongings at the station.

"Mr. Blue, where is your identification? Do you have a driver's license or some sort of identification?"

"I do," Shorty said. "Just check my wallet. I don't have any warrants or felonies. I have a clean record. I've been working on the streets all morning. I don't go into peoples' houses."

"Well, we got some questions to ask you and it is important you clear things up," the officer said.

"What's to clear up?" Shorty asked. "You searched me and I don't have anything."

"Well, the product could be at your house, so we need to take you in and get a search warrant," the officer replied. "Where do you live?"

"45th and Avalon Boulevard," Shorty responded. "Off the alley in a backhouse. I live alone with my dog."

The officers helped Shorty into the back of the police cruiser. "OK," the officer said. "Let's take him to the station."

The officers drove Shorty, his dog and belongings to the local precinct where he was booked for burglary and grand theft. Shorty sat in the murky, gray cell underneath the building and thought about the mess he was in. California was a community property state, so for him to be jailed for burglary circumstantially was racial profiling. He was in the area, but there was no proof that he burglarized any property. Shorty was given a chance to make a phone call or accept a public defender awarded by the court. Since he was held on a felony count, he would be in jail for a week.

Shorty was miserable. He had never been to jail before and felt helpless. He didn't want to call Phoebe because then she and Booker would know where he was and he didn't want either of them meddling in his business. He decided to wait for the public defender.

Later that afternoon a public defender by the name of Richard Wayne arrived. He was a tall, dark-skinned Black man in a brown suit. Mr. Wayne was carrying a leather briefcase. Shorty introduced himself and Mr. Wayne did the same; he seemed interested in Shorty's case and what Shorty had to say. Mr. Wayne asked Shorty if he had money for a private attorney to assist with the case, which made Shorty uneasy.

Why would he ask a question like that, Shorty wondered? *Could it be that the amount of money the state pays him is not enough for him to do a good job? Is he really interested in my case? Time will tell.* One thing Shorty knew for certain: this whole situation didn't make any sense.

"Why would I commit a burglary?" Shorty asked.

"Street people often break into houses out of desperation," Mr. Wayne responded.

"Well, I did not do it. Let's go through the process and I will prove to you that I didn't have to steal from anybody."

"You mean you are rich?" Mr. Wayne asked.

"What does being rich have to do with it?" Shorty questioned. "I've got morals and money. People are so treacherous that you cannot be flamboyant and wealthy these days. I have a sister back in Mississippi whose husband started a fight with me because they wanted the deed to my part of the family property. When people know you've got something they don't have, and they want, they will try to take it away from you, any way they can. Does that make sense, Mr. Wayne?"

"So your family tried to set you up," Mr. Wayne asked.

"Sure they did," Shorty said.

"Well I know you surely don't sound like a transient man or uneducated for that matter," Mr. Wayne said.

"If I was running around here in a fancy car wearing mohair suits. I would not have anything for long," Shorty said. "I would be broke with no future."

"I understand Mr. Blue," the lawyer said. "Let's see about bailing you out. You can come back for the arraignment. You don't have a criminal history, right?"

"Of course I don't," Shorty said. "That's why I stayed away from certain people most of my life. I want to be loved and I want someone to want me for me, not what I have or can do for them. It's about the pursuit of the truth. The people accusing me of stealing are liars and the truth is not in them."

Shorty was arraigned on Tuesday morning and released. He was ordered to return in a month.

"Mr. Blue, I need more information from you." Attorney Wayne said a few weeks after Shorty was released. "I need more information about you for your deposition."

"This is too stressful," Shorty said.

"We need a clear biography of who you are on paper," Mr. Wayne said.

"I am a rubbish collector," Shorty started. "I collect things that seem to have no value and trade or sell it on the open market. I'm not a transient. I have assets. I maintain a low profile because of what my family attempted to do to me. After a family inheritance left by my mother, my sister's husband beat me up and tried to kill me for my deed to the property. If my own family would be that money hungry, what makes me think people who are strangers won't do the same?"

"So Shorty, are you broke?" Mr. Wayne asked.

"No, I am not broke. I can hire a private attorney to represent me, if there is a problem," Shorty said. "I didn't do anything. I have no motive to steal from anyone."

"Why would I not believe you Mr. Blue?" Wayne asked. "I know how the system works. I know they want to make the fall guy."

"That's right; they will convict me and it would be years before the truth comes out," Shorty said. "That's why I need to fight this now. I don't have years of my life to give away for something I didn't do."

Attorney Wayne collected all the information he needed from Shorty. Shorty had to present his bank statements and information on his assets, which made him uneasy. Shorty was reluctant to reveal his estate. He eventually told Mr. Wayne about his oil well, but the attorney didn't believe him.

"If you have what you say you have, then you would not be doing what you are doing. Why work for a restaurant cooking hamburgers when you could own the restaurant?" Mr. Wayne rationalized. "Shorty, what you are saying doesn't make any sense."

"When the time comes, I'll prove what I say," Shorty said, before hanging up the phone.

Chapter

29

R . Lee Walker

Shorty was starting to have reoccurring dreams of his mother. In the dreams, his mother advised him to hide his money and that he would have to expose his finances to keep him out of trouble. She warned him of women who only wanted what he had to give them; she beckoned for him to be safe. Shorty woke the next day from the dream a bit dazed, yet even more focused on his court date. He wanted to ensure he could beat the case and move on with his life.

Eventually, Shorty returned to business as usual. While checking the cans on 54th Street and Central Avenue, he saw another man pushing a cart with a dog. The man waved at Shorty and Shorty waved back. The man approached Shorty wearing a gray khaki suit and brown work boots.

"My name is Charlie Wilson and this is my dog, Chester," the man said.

"I'm Shorty and this is my dog, Buster," Shorty said. "Nice to meet you."

"How long have you been around these parts of the city?" Charlie asked. "I've never seen you before."

"I am new to this area but not new enough to not get in trouble," Shorty said. "LAPD is trying to frame me with burglary."

"Shorty, let's go somewhere we can talk," Charlie said. "I can tell there's a lot you don't know. Come on and follow me. We need to talk."

Charlie and Shorty walked over to behind the liquor store on Central and 8th Avenues.

"Listen Shorty, I'm 73 years old and I know the game," Charlie said. "I know some of the secrets you are living already. Do you want something to drink?"

"No, I'm fine," Shorty said.

"Shorty, I've been a millionaire in South Central for years," Charlie continued. "I live in disguise. I don't knock nobody. I live in a little room and own a rental property. When I turn 75, I'm going to sell my property to rid myself of these headaches with taxes and repairs. As your money builds, open up an account in a small town outside of Los Angeles. When you go to make deposits, wear clean clothes. In this city, the less people you talk to the better. Most women out here will set you up, if you let them. There is no love. I recommend you pay for sex. Do I make sense so far? Be your own person. Stay away from crazy people who will raise your temper. Your own family can be your own worst enemy."

Shorty was taken aback by how similar his story was to Charlie's. He was starting to get a bit nervous and apprehensive. The more Charlie talked, Shorty began to realize the streets took a toll on the old man mentally. Charlie's conversation would switch from business to food within seconds. "Don't drink orange juice, buy fresh oranges ... don't eat sick apples or sick fruit ... doctors will kill you ... let nature heal you ... the only time you are sick is when you have stomach problems." Charlie ended his argument by simply telling Shorty to stay out of trouble and to keep to himself. Shorty felt as if he was getting schooled in Life 101.

"It is time for you to go Shorty," Charlie said. "I've told you everything you need to know. I'll see you around." And with that, Charlie and his dog left.

Shortly after his run-in with Charlie, Shorty began to withdraw money from his accounts to help churches and homeless shelters in the area. He felt no one should have to live on the streets and would donate large amounts of money anonymously to any shelter he stayed at that treated him well. In 30 days, Shorty's court date came around. He arrived on time, dressed in a blue business suit, to Department 85. The prosecuting attorney delivered circumstantial evidence and the police report.

As the judge listened, the court clerk walked into the room to deliver a file. She recognized Shorty and asked the clerk of the room what the charges were. Once the visiting clerk heard of the charges, she said, "The trash is picked up on Wednesday around that time where I live. After I walk my kids to school, I catch the bus and see that man at the same location with his dog. So for him to be on the other side of town when it is not trash day makes no sense. Tell his attorney I will be an independent witness for Mr. Shorty Blue." Attorney Wayne submitted Shorty Blue's financial information – which the court found surprising and almost unbelievable – along with the advent of an independent witness. The judge found that the charges against Shorty Blue were unfounded and based on insufficient evidence. The case was dismissed.

Back in Mississippi, Booker was preparing to travel to California. He had got word that Shorty was in trouble and was determined to get out there to get back what was due to him and Phoebe. He knew that black folk stayed in centralized areas, so finding Shorty wouldn't be a problem. He knew that once in Los Angeles, he would go to the black neighborhood and ask around. Somebody would have information to give him in locating Shorty.

Booker arrived in Los Angeles and quickly found the area where the black people lived. Booker had a picture of Shorty and started asking around to see if anyone knew him. Most people didn't know him; however, when he asked around South Park on Avalon Avenue, he got some leads. Booker walked up and down Avalon Avenue and stopped at a mechanic's shop. He asked the man if he had seen Shorty. The mechanic nodded affirmatively and told Booker that Shorty lives in the alley behind the liquor store in a garage with his dog. This was the big break Booker needed.

Booker went over to the spot and cased Shorty's place. He waited until evening and hid outside until Shorty came home. As soon as Shorty walked in and closed the door, Booker shot through the window three times and ran. To the neighbors, the gunshots sounded like a car backfiring; the police weren't called. Booker went to the nearest payphone and called Phoebe to let her know he shot Shorty and that her brother was now dead. When Phoebe heard the news, she became sad and her conscience wouldn't let her rest. Shorty was in his living room, laying in a puddle of blood, as Buster barked continuously.

Shorty's neighbors came out and saw that his truck was parked at a time when Shorty is usually out and about. They went inside and called the paramedics. Once the paramedics arrived, they busted down the door and found Shorty on the floor. He wasn't dead but he was barely breathing. Shorty was rushed to General Hospital where they were able to save his life. Meanwhile in Mississippi, Phoebe's conscience had wiped her out. She was so distraught and had cried so much that she went to the police and told them what Booker did to her brother. A few days later, once Booker returned to Mississippi by train, he was arrested at the docking station for attempted murder. Shorty later recovered and went back to picking up rubbish on Central Avenue. On Sundays, he cleaned up and went to Trinity Baptist Church where he met the lady from the shelter. They became friends and lovers. The oil wells went dry and he pulled all his money from his accounts. Shorty always maintained his garage apartment. He was a good man and when he died, he died peacefully in his sleep.

As time passed Shorty had forgiven his sisters for their wrongdoings and he had helped them out by sending them each a check for $50,000. He also gave his lady friend and lover a check for the same amount. All his remaining money was found in his mattress... Over $2 million dollars, most of which later went to a medical fellowship for minority doctors.

Epilogue

R . Lee Walker

Shorty Blue lived and died peacefully. He never had to go to the hospital, except for when Booker shot him. He never got a cold or any aches and pains from getting old., Most people liked Shorty Blue. He was not a bad guy. He stayed off to himself and just took care of his business.

The community missed seeing Shorty Blue. A lot of people did not know who he was although he was a regular on Central Avenue in South Central. He was never seen talking to or laughing with people, so most suspected he had good sense. His clothes were clean and most people didn't know he had a truck to dump the cans and bottles in. Shorty knew the community; he was up before dawn. Fortunately for him, he was never robbed or assaulted, even though he didn't trust banks and kept his money in his mattress. He did give much of his money away. He liked giving it to sustain people. He felt his blessings would come from God and they did.

R . Lee Walker

About The Author

R. Lee Walker

R. Lee Walker was born in Prentiss, Mississippi. He moved to Los Angeles, California with his parents. His mother Louvatter, grandmother Alberta, and grandfather Leroy Walker. He graduated from California State University at Dominguez Hills. Later, he completed graduate work at the University of California at Los Angeles.

Mr. Walker worked in Corporate America for many years and finished his career in criminal justice. He has written several books, "Paprika Version of Wisdom". "Passion for Life Reason to Live", and "Too Good To Be Used." He has traveled the world and speaks several languages.

Mr. Walker lives with his family in Los Angeles.

R. Lee Walker

Shorty
Blue
A Novel

Shorty Blue is an ingenious fictitious story that covers the dynamics of human interactions when a loved-one dies. The story explores the rivalry and conflicts that family members face with issues that may go unresolved for years.

I challenge you to enjoy this fascinating
journey in human emotions. This story may
someday be considered an urban classic.
– R. Lee Walker

R. Lee Walker worked in Corporate America for many years and finished his career in criminal justice. Mr. Walker has written several books, "Paprika Version of Wisdom," "Passion for Life Reason to Live," and "Too Good To Be Used."

Printed in the United States
by Baker & Taylor Publisher Services